For Colin, Hank, and Milo Meloy, with love

First edition 2015. Library of Congress Catalog Card Number 2014931830. ISBN 978-0-7636-6529-6.
This book was hand-lettered by the author. The illustrations were done in gouache and ink.
Candlewick Press, 99 Dover Street, Somerville, Massachusetts 02144. visit us at www.candlewick.com.
Printed in Shenzhen, Guangdong, China. 14 15 16 17 18 19 CCP 10 9 8 7 6 5 4 3 2 1

Home

Carson Ellis

CANDLEWICK PRESS

Home is a house in the country.

Or home is an apartment.

Some homes are boats.

Some homes are wigwams.

Some are palaces.

Or underground lairs.

Or shoes.

French people live in French homes.

Atlantians make their homes underwater.

And some folks live on the road.

Clean homes. Messy homes.

Tall homes.

Short homes.

Sea homes.

Bee homes.

Hollow
tree homes.

But whose home is this?

And what about this?

Who in the world lives here?

And why?

This is the home of a Slovakian duchess.

This is the home of a Kenyan blacksmith.

This is the home of a Japanese businessman.

This is the home of a Norse god.

A babushka lives here.

A Moonian lives here.

A raccoon lives here.

An artist lives here.

This is my home,
and this is me.

Where is your home?
Where are you?